JUST GO TO BED

BY MERCER MAYER

SCHOLASTIC INC.

New York Toronto London Auckland Sydney
Mexico City New Delhi Hong Kong Buenos Aires

I'm a cowboy and
I round up cows.
I can lasso anything.

Dad says…

"It's time for the cowboy to come inside and get ready for bed."

I'm a general and I have to stop the enemy army with my tank.

Dad says…

"It's time for the general to take a bath."

I'm a space cadet and I zoom
to the moon.

I capture a robot
with my ray gun.

Dad says…

"This giant robot has captured the space cadet and is going to put him in the bathtub right now."

Dad says, "It's time for the
sea monster to have a snack."

I'm a zookeeper feeding
my hungry animals.

Dad says…

"Feeding time is over. Here are
the zookeeper's pajamas."

I'm Super Critter flying over the city.

I'm a train engineer being chased by bandits.

Dad says,
"The bandit chief
has caught you
so put on
your pajamas."

But I'm a race car driver
and I just speed away.

Dad says, "The race is over.
Now put on these pajamas
and go to bed."

I'm a bunny hopping around my garden.

Dad says...

"But I'm a bunny and bunnies don't sleep in a bed."

Mom says, "Shhh!"
Dad says, "Go to sleep."

Well, maybe a tired bunny
could sleep in a bed...

just this once.